P9-DHP-214

This book
belongs to:

_____

MESSAGE TO PARENTS

This book is perfect for parents and children to read aloud together. First read the story to your child. When you read it again run your finger under each line, stopping at each picture for your child to "read." Help your child to figure out the picture. If your child makes a mistake, be encouraging as you say the right word. Point out the written word beneath each picture in the margin on the page. Soon your child will be "reading" aloud with you, and at the same time learning the symbols that stand for words.

Copyright © 1988 Checkerboard Press, Inc. All rights reserved.
READ ALONG WITH ME books are conceived by Deborah Shine.
READ ALONG WITH ME and its logo are trademarks of Checkerboard Press, Inc.
Library of Congress Catalog Card Number: 88-25709 ISBN: 002-898135-9
Printed in the United States of America 0 9 8 7 6 5 4

Checkerboard Press, Inc.
30 Vesey Street, New York, New York 10007

Happy Birthday, Roger

A Read Along With Me Book

By Cindy West

Illustrated by Olivia Cole

CHECKERBOARD PRESS
NEW YORK

Roger

Jenny

Sam

Rags

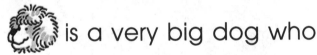 is a very big dog who

lives with his friends  and

 and a mischievous cat

named  .

One morning  woke up

feeling especially excited – it was

his birthday. 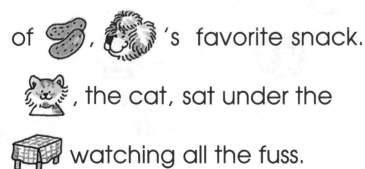 and 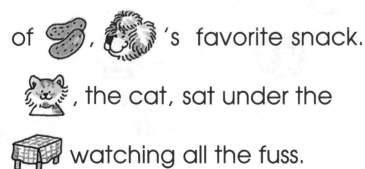 helped to make a birthday .

They also prepared a big

of , 's favorite snack.

, the cat, sat under the

 watching all the fuss.

cake

dish

pickles

table

Jenny

Roger

Rags

pickle

gift

She watched as  tied a

ribbon on  and gave him a

big hug. felt jealous.

Suddenly  thought of a

sneaky plan – a plan to make

 miss his birthday party!

 grabbed a and tied

a ribbon to it. Then she dragged

the outside.

"Oh, !" called .

"Here's a birthday  for you!"

But as 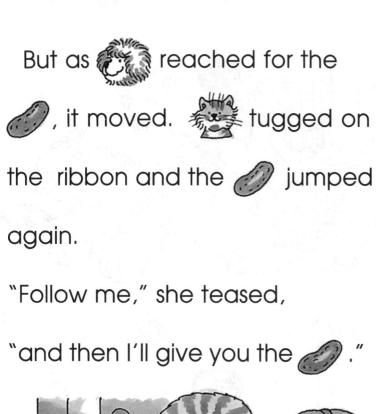 reached for the

, it moved. tugged on

the ribbon and the jumped

again.

"Follow me," she teased,

"and then I'll give you the ."

Rags

pickle

Roger

 pulled the down the street, and trotted eagerly after her. He didn't notice all the children and their dogs coming to his party.

 ran far out into the country. ran after her. stopped

in front of a , dropped the

, and ran off.

 gobbled up the  as

quickly as he could. Then he

looked around – and when all he

saw was a  and a field of

,  knew he was lost.

barn

corn

pickle

Roger

Rags

"Now I'm really in a  !" groaned. "I'll miss my party."

Meanwhile, , who never ever, ever got lost, ran home.

All the  told 🧒 and 🧑 how 🐱 had led 🦁 away with a 🥔 . "That was a very naughty thing to do" scolded 🧑 .

Meanwhile, 🦁 was feeling more and more lost. He ran past a big 🐄 , and a lot of pink 🐷 and a field full of watermelons, but 🦁 couldn't find his house. Then he saw a 👨 , so he rushed toward him barking.

children

Jenny

Sam

cow

pigs

man

man

bow

Roger

"You're frisky, aren't you?"

said the  . "And your

is so smart. The  read the

tag on  's collar.

"Hmm, I see your name is

and you live pretty far away.

That means you're lost!"

"Woof!"  answered.

"Well," said the , "jump into

my , and I'll drive you home."

truck

truck

Roger

As the rocked and rumbled and sped along, 🦔 tumbled around with the watermelons! It was great fun!

Back at 🦔's house everyone was worried.

"I think 🦔 is really lost," said

sadly. But just then, everyone

saw the big stop outside the

. Loud, happy barking was

coming from the back. Out jumped

 – with lots of watermelons!

Sam

house

Roger

Jenny

Sam

" , you're back!" exclaimed

 and . They rushed over

and hugged him.

"Now we can have your party!"

 shouted happily.

But just as they were about to

sing "Happy Birthday,"

Rags

chair

pickle

noticed sitting sadly under

a , all alone.

"What's the matter?" asked 🧒.

"Are you sad because it's 🦁's

birthday? Is that why you tricked

him with the ?"

Rags

Sam

cake

 nodded her head.

"Well," told her, "when

your birthday comes, you'll have

a party and a birthday with a

gift too. " Everyone helped

feel like she was an important

guest at the party.

perked up her ears and

began to purr. She felt so happy

she helped blow out the birthday

candles.

", what did you wish for?"

 asked.

"I know what he wished for –

 !"  laughed.

And a jar of  was the very

first  he got!

Roger

Jenny

pickles

gift